MW00414880

Moon Rocks
and
Dinosaur Bones

By Nancy I. Sanders and
Susan Titus Osborn

Illustrated by Julie Durrell

With love for my cousin Laura. May you learn more about Jesus through reading this book. — S.T.O.

With love for Stephanie Shaner. May you continue to use the gifts God has given you for His purpose and glory. — N.I.S.

Parables in Action Series

Lost and Found
Hidden Treasure
Comet Campout
Moon Rocks and Dinosaur Bones

Text copyright © 1999 Nancy I. Sanders and Susan Titus Osborn
Illustrations copyright © 1999 Concordia Publishing House
3558 S. Jefferson Avenue, St. Louis, MO 63118-3968
Manufactured in the United States of America

2 3 4 5 6 7 8 9 10   08 07 06 05 04 03 02 01 00

Hi! My name is Suzie. Today
Mario, The Spy, and I are having
a good-bye party for Bubbles.
She is blasting off in a spaceship. She will fly to the moon!

Bubbles does ads on TV. Her new ad is for Razzle Dazzle Rockets. The toy company wants her to zoom to the moon in the TV ad.

"Cool spacesuit!" I said to Bubbles.

"Mumph moo," Bubbles said.

I think she said *thank you*. I couldn't hear her. She wore a glass helmet. It looked like a bubble.

"When is Bubbles leaving?" Mario asked.

"In an hour," I said. Bubbles nodded her helmet. The Spy wrote in his spy book.

"I'm leaving right now," Mario said. "My dad's taking me to a show for people who collect rocks. I want to find a special rock. I'll add it to my collection."

Mario reached in his pocket. "I found more dinosaur bones at my empty lot. These are little bones. But they're still worth money."

Earlier, Mario found two whole dinosaurs. Their bones were buried in his empty lot. He gave the dinosaurs to the museum.

"I have to leave now," Mario said. "I don't have time to put these bones in a safe place." He looked at the three of us. "Will you keep them safe for me?"

We nodded. Mario gave me one of the bones. He gave The Spy a bone. Bubbles reached out her astronaut glove. Mario put a bone in her glove. He held up the last bone.

"What will I do with this one?" he asked.

I pointed to a small table. "Put it there. We'll keep it safe."

"Thanks," said Mario. He gave a high five to Bubbles. "Have fun on the moon!"

"Mumph moo," Bubbles said inside her helmet.

"Bye!" We all waved as Mario ran out the door.

"Take care of Woof too!" Mario shouted as he left. Woof wagged his tail. "WOOF!"

Then the phone rang. Br-r-ring! I picked it up. It was for Bubbles. The lady on the phone said, "This is Mrs. Miller. Tell Bubbles I'm sorry."

"Sorry about what?" I asked.

"I'm sorry I can't pay for her trip to the moon," said Mrs. Miller.

I hung up the phone. I told Bubbles what Mrs. Miller said.

The Spy wrote lots of notes in his book.

Bubbles talked inside her helmet. "What?" I asked. "I can't hear you."

I watched Bubbles' mouth
move. "What?" I asked again.
"Do you need money to fly to
the moon?"

Bubbles reached up. She
took off her helmet. "I have to
raise money for my trip. Mrs.
Miller said she'd pay my way.
Now I don't have enough
money. I can't go to the moon.
What will I do?"

Wow! Things looked pretty
bad. Bubbles just HAD to go
to the moon! It would be so
exciting!

I looked at the dinosaur bone
in my hand. I thought a minute.

Then I had an idea. "We can sell the bones to the museum. Then we'll have money for your trip."

"We can't sell the dinosaur bones," Bubbles said. "They're Mario's!"

The Spy looked up from writing his spy notes. He said, "Blem."

I knew what THAT meant. I'd been around The Spy a long time. "Blem" was a secret code for "Let's pray." The Spy liked to talk in secret code.

We all prayed together. We asked Jesus to help us do the right thing.

15

"I think Mario would WANT us to sell the bones," I said. "He'd want Bubbles to zoom to the moon. He knows how important it is."

The Spy nodded his head. He wrote down more notes in his book. Then he handed me his dinosaur bone.

Bubbles looked at the bone in her glove. She handed it to me. "You're the best friends anyone could have," she said.

I looked at the table. Where was the other bone? It was missing! Suddenly I realized that Woof was missing too. Where was Woof?

"Oh, no!" Bubbles cried. "Woof took the other dinosaur bone!"

The Spy looked at his spy watch.

"We don't have much time," I said. "Let's run to the museum. We'll sell these three bones. Then you can get on the space-ship."

Bubbles carried her helmet. We all ran out the door. We headed for the museum. We ran past Mario's empty lot.

"There's Woof!" I cried.

Woof wagged his tail and barked. "WOOF! WOOF! WOOF!"

"Oh, no!" Bubbles cried. "Woof buried Mario's bone. Now we'll never find it."

"That's okay," I said. "Mario will understand. He'll know it was a mistake. Come on!"

Woof followed us to the museum. We sold the bones. Now we had enough money! We hurried to the spaceship. Crowds of people stood everywhere.

Bubbles snapped on her helmet.

The Spy wrote spy notes. Woof barked. "WOOF!"

I hugged Bubbles good-bye. "I'm praying for a safe trip," I said.

"Mumph moo," she said inside her helmet.

Bubbles climbed into the spaceship.

"Larry! Susan!" It was Mr. Zinger. Mr. Zinger is our teacher. He always calls us by our real names. The Spy's real name is Larry. Mine is Susan.

"I'm glad I got here in time," Mr. Zinger said. "Imagine! Flying to the moon!"

The countdown started: 10, 9, 8, 7, 6, 5, 4, 3, 2, 1! Blast off!

Everyone cheered, "Hip, hip, hooray!"

We watched the spaceship go up. Up, up, up it went. Soon it was a small dot in the sky. Then we watched it on a special TV.

We saw Bubbles inside the spaceship. She held up a toy. It was a new Razzle Dazzle Rocket. We all clapped.

Bubbles waved to everyone. She floated upside down. She did cart-wheels and flips in the air. Wow!

Zoom! Zoom! Zoom! We watched the spaceship on TV. It zoomed to the moon. Then it landed.

The door opened. Out stepped Bubbles. Everyone cheered again.

Bubbles walked on the moon in her spacesuit.

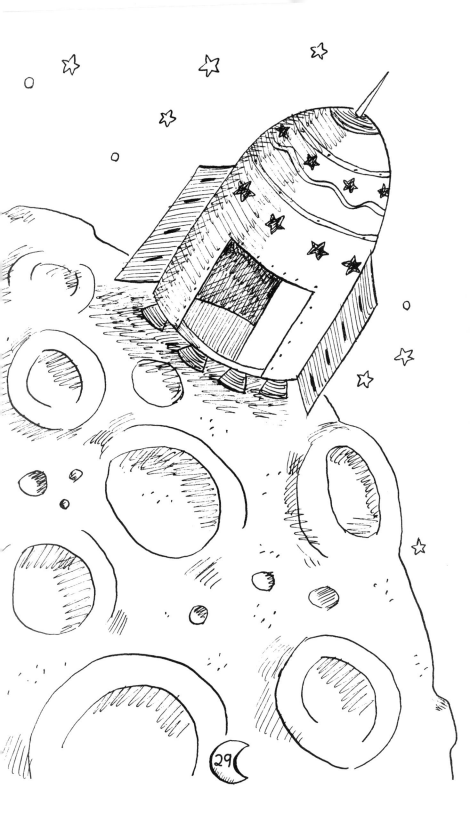

29

Bubbles reached down. She picked up something from the moon. She put it in her pocket. What was it?

Bubbles walked back to the spaceship. She waved. Then she climbed back into the spaceship.

Zoom! Zoom! Zoom! The spaceship zoomed back home. Then it landed.

The door opened. Out walked Bubbles. Bubbles waved to the crowd.

Everyone cheered. What a fun day!

The next morning, the phone rang.

"Hi, Suzie," Mario said. "I'm back from my show. I didn't find any special rocks."

"That's too bad," I said.
"Listen, Mario." I wanted to tell
him about the bones.

"I can't listen now," he said.
"My dad needs the phone. Meet
me at the empty lot. Bring the
bones."

The bones? We didn't have the bones.

We sold the bones! What should we do?

I ran out the door.

I ran to the empty lot.

Bubbles and The Spy were already there. So were Mario and Woof.

"Why are you still wearing a spacesuit?" I asked Bubbles.

Bubbles reached up and took off her helmet. "Razzle Dazzle Rockets just took my picture. I was holding a moon rock."

"Wow!" Mario said. "I watched your trip on TV. They had TVs everywhere at the show."

"Thanks," Bubbles said with a smile.

"Now about the bones ..." I began.

"That's right," Mario said. "Thanks for keeping the bones safe. I'll take them back now."

I looked at Bubbles.

Bubbles looked at me.

I looked at The Spy. He was busy writing notes in his spy book.

I took a deep breath.

"We sold the bones to the museum," I said.

Bubbles and I told Mario the whole story.

Then Bubbles reached into her pocket. She pulled out a small gray rock.

"Here, Mario," said Bubbles. "This rock is for you."

"WOW!" Mario shouted. He started jumping up and down. "That's a moon rock!"

Bubbles grinned. "They said I could keep it after they took my picture. I want to give it to you to add to your collection."

"Super!" Mario said. "Thanks! I'm glad you sold the bones. The money helped Bubbles make her trip. Now I have the best rock EVER."

I said a quick prayer. I thanked Jesus for helping us. We HAD done the right thing.

Suddenly Woof started barking. "WOOF! WOOF! WOOF!"

We all ran over to Woof. He was digging a hole.

"Look!" I cried. "It's the other dinosaur bone!"

"Woof must have buried it here," Bubbles said. "I'm glad we found it again." She snapped on her helmet.

"It's not worth anything lying here," Mario said. He picked up the small bone. "Let's raise money for another special project."

Parable of the Loaned Money

Based on Matthew 25:14–30

Jesus told a parable:

A man went on a trip. He left his money behind with his three servants.

One servant hid the money. The other servants used their money wisely.

When the man came back, he was happy with the servants who used his money wisely.

Mario went on a trip too. He
left his dinosaur bones with his
friends. Woof buried one bone in

a hole. Mario's friends, however, wisely sold their bones to the museum so Bubbles could go to the moon.

When Mario came back, he was happy his friends had used the bones for doing something good.

God has given special gifts to each one of us. These gifts are called talents. God wants us to use our talents wisely. We can use them to help people learn about Jesus and His love.

Hi!
What special talents has God given to you? How can you use these talents to share the love of Jesus with others? Here's one way you can put Jesus' Parable of the Loaned Money into ACTION!

Parables In Action

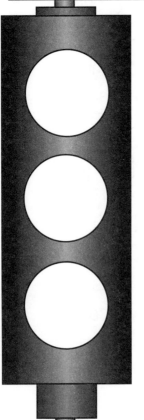

Get Ready. Team up with your friends at church to hold a talent show. Pray for the kids who will come to watch.

Get Set. You and your friends can practice using the talents God gave each of you. Sing a song about Jesus. Prepare a short play about a Bible story. Play "Jesus Loves Me" on a keyboard

Go! Hold a talent show in your yard for all the neighborhood kids. Use your talents to tell them about Jesus and His love.

48